School of Meanies

Daren King
Illustrations by David Roberts

Quercus

First published in Great Britain in 2011 by

Quercus
21 Bloomsbury Square
London
WC1A 2NS

A CIP catalogue reference for this book is available
from the British Library

ISBN 978 0 85738 382 2

10 9 8 7 6 5 4 3 2

Printed and bound in Great Britain by Clays Ltd, St Ives plc.

School of Meanies

Daren King studied in Bath and lives in London. *Mouse Noses on Toast*, his first book for children, won the Gold Nestlé Children's Prize. *Peter the Penguin Pioneer* was shortlisted for the Blue Peter Award. He is the author of four adult books. *Boxy an Star* was shortlisted for the Guardian First Book Award.

David Roberts is the award-winning illustrator of over thirty titles. He has had a variety of interesting jobs, such as hair washer, shelf stacker, and hat designer. He was born in Liverpool and now lives in London.

Praise for Daren King

'I loved all the ghosties' beautifully sketched characteristics, and the sensitive way in which King's story helps children understand fear: a "wibbly feeling in the tummy"' *Daily Telegraph*

'King is very good at making children think about their world . . . hugely inventive and charmingly funny, early readers will adore having this book read to them and will love trying it themselves'
Literary Review

'Full of fun, humour and ridiculous behaviour'
My Child

'Children will laugh out loud at the zany humour and the witty one-liners . . . while David Roberts' comical illustrations can't fail to raise a giggle'
Scholastic Litera

'Writer and illustrate
fun-pac

Contents

1
Ghost School

Ghost School is boring. You get told off for bumping!

Bumping is my best thing. The only thing I like better than bumping is cake and lollipops, and the only thing I like better than cake and lollipops is bumping a box of cake and lollipops, and—

'Humphrey!'

It was Tabitha Tumbly. Tabitha is the youngest grown-up ghosty and the nicest of the lot – no fibbing!

'Humphrey Bump, what happened to that box of cake and lollipops?'

'The cat bumped it,' I said. 'I mean, the cat knocked it over, with her paws.'

Tabitha folded her arms and frowned at the upside-down cardboard box, and the lollipops scattered across the kitchen tiles and the splodged cake.

'Humphrey, are you fibbing?'

'No,' I said. 'I mean, yes. I mean, I don't know.'

We were in the kitchen at the back of the house, just me and Tabitha, and it was a school day but I didn't want to go.

'Put your blazer on,' Tabitha said. 'I'll float you to school.'

I looked at where I'd left my blazer in a heap on the kitchen table. 'I'm not going to school today.'

'But it's your first day back.'

'That's why I'm not going. The first day back is horrible.'

My blazer floated off the table and hovered behind me like a bat. Tabitha is a poltergeist. She can move things with her powers. No fibbing!

'Why don't you like the first day?' Tabitha asked as I poked my arms into the blazer.

'It's horrible. You haven't seen the other children all summer, and then you have to see them – and they make fun of you because you're fat!'

'Children can be so mean,' Wither said, floating in from the garden. 'And, Humphrey, you're not fat. You're just, er, overly proportioned.'

Wither is a poet. That's why nothing he says makes any sense.

'Come along, Humphrey,' Tabitha said, floating into the hall. 'We'd better wisp, or you'll be late.'

'I'll wisp with you,' said Wither.
'It's a lovely day for a wisp, and I need to
stretch my transparent bits.'

Ghost School used to be a still-alive school,
in the old days, but then it got run down, so the
still-alives built a new school on the other side
of the village.

'Wait,' I said as Ghost School loomed into
view. 'I have to tie my shoelaces.' And I wisped
behind an old oak tree and hid.

'Humphrey?' Tabitha said, floating back and
forth. 'Humphrey, where did you go?'

'There's nobody here,' I said in a sort of tree
voice. 'Just us trees, and—'

The two grown-up ghosties peered around
the trunk, and Tabitha took my hand and led
me back to the path.

'You'll be fine when you get there and
see your friends waiting for you,' Wither
said.

'I haven't got any friends,' I said. 'Everyone hates me.'

But then I spotted Samuel Spook and Phil and Fay Phantom flitting across the playground, and I let go of Tabitha's hand and bounced off through the school gates.

2

Haunted Homework

'Ghost School is stupid and rubbish, and, um, I'm not going to Ghost School ever again!'

I'd practised saying that all the way home, but then I saw Tabitha and Agatha chopping vegetables in the kitchen, and the words bounced about inside my head, and when I opened my mouth nothing came out.

'Humphrey, how was your first day back at Ghost School?' Tabitha asked as carrots rolled across the chopping board.

'It was, um, fun,' I said, bobbing by the stove.

'Dinner will be ready soon,' Tabitha said. 'Pie, with your favourite side helping of sausages, pie, sausage pie, chips, pie and pizza.'

'Us girls are having salad,' Agatha said, biting a pointy, pointless carrot.

'I'm not hungry,' I said, even though my tummy felt like a cave.

'That's not like you,' Pamela said, emerging from the larder, her arms piled up with plates. Pamela Fraidy is always nervous, so the plates rattled and clanged.

'Humphrey,' Agatha said as I floated out to the hall, 'you look as if you've found a lollipop and dropped it.'

On the stairs I floated past Wither and Charlie Vapour. Charlie winked at me and took off his hat.

'Master Bump,' Wither said, 'Charlie doffed his trilby, and you didn't so much as bid him good day.'

'I did the polite thing to do,' Charlie said. 'The least you can do, Humphrey, is do the polite thing to do too.'

'But it isn't a good day,' I said, bumping the banister. 'It's a rotten day, with knobs on.'

'Don't be mean,' said Wither, pursing his lips.

'Humphrey is sulking,' Charlie said. 'Today was the first day back at school. He'll feel right as rain tomorrow.'

At the top of the stairs I bumped through the bedroom door, then bumped it closed behind me. I had my own bedroom now that the still-alives had moved out. The grown-up ghosties shared the four-poster bed in their old room.

I rummaged through my blazer pockets

and pulled out a fluffy doughnut. I was halfway through munching it when I heard Charlie and Tabitha talking on the landing.

'I don't know what's got into him,' Tabitha was saying. 'He used to love Ghost School. Have a word with him, Charlie.'

'You talk to him, Tabitha. You're closer to him in age. Humphrey won't listen to an old duffer like me.'

'But you're a man, Charlie. All boys

together! And you can pass through. In you float!'

Charlie Vapour can pass through doors and walls and, well, anything – even when he's got his hat on. I'm not telling fibs!

I'd just taken another bite of the doughnut when Charlie's head passed through the bedroom door.

Charlie winked at me and doffed his hat. 'Are you alright, son?' he said in his cockney accent.

I nodded. I had my mouth full.

'Glad to hear it,' Charlie said, and he passed back.

The door handle turned by itself – Tabitha using her powers again – and Tabitha floated into the room.

'Humphrey, I've brought you a snack,' Tabitha said, and she dropped a crusty pork pie onto the bed.

'That wouldn't feed a mouse.'

Tabitha smiled, sort of kind but telling me off at the same time. 'If you want your dinner, you will have to float to the kitchen.'

'I'm not hungry,' I fibbed.

'Then there really is something wrong. Either you're coming down with flu, or something happened at school and you're afraid to say what.'

'Nothing happened at school,' I said. 'I'm just doing my homework, that's all.'

'If that's true, the homework must be haunted and see-through,' Tabitha said, 'because all I can see are doughnut crumbs and a grumpy face.'

I looked up at Tabitha's big eyes and said, 'Tabitha, if I tell you something, do you promise not to be cross?'

Tabitha sat beside me on the bed. Well,

floated. Ghosties can't sit on things, they can only float above things.

'I got expelled,' I told her. 'I've been thrown out of Ghost School. For good.'

3

The Ghost
Headmaster

After breakfast next morning, Tabitha Tumbly
and Charlie Vapour wisped me straight to the
Ghost Headmaster's office.

Charlie knocked on the door with his
knuckles, doffed his hat – the polite thing to
do, no fibbing! – and passed through the
wood.

'Let's leave Charlie to it,' I said, and I tried

to wisp out of the window but Tabitha snapped
her fingers and the window slammed
shut.

The door to the Ghost Headmaster's office
opened, and Charlie was there in the doorway.
He looked like he'd seen a ghost.

'Best manners,' Charlie whispered into my
ear as Tabitha and me floated into the office.
'The Headmaster is in a bad mood.'

'He's always in a bad mood,' I said.

The Ghost Headmaster floated by the
window with his back to us. He wore his flowing
black cape and that hat like a black sandwich
with a bit of lettuce hanging off it.

'Close the door,' the Ghost Headmaster said in his vaporous voice, and the door slammed closed and Tabitha looked at me and winked. 'Right,' the Ghost Headmaster said, wisping round, 'what's all this about?'

'Um,' Charlie said, hiding behind his hat.

'Humphrey is a pupil here at Ghost School,' Tabitha said. 'At least, he was.'

'Ah, the Rotund Rascal,' the Ghost Headmaster said with a smiling moustache. 'That's what the teachers call the boy. Humphrey Bump, the Rotund Rascal.'

'I'm not a rascal,' I said, my voice shaking. 'I just bump a lot, for fun.'

'Yes,' the Ghost Headmaster said. 'And, thus, expulsion.'

Charlie frowned. 'If only Wither were here,' he whispered. 'Wither understands all that poetic talk.'

'What the Ghost Headmaster is saying,'

Tabitha whispered, 'is that the reason poor little Humphrey got expelled is because he bumps.'

'Always bounding about,' the Ghost Headmaster said as he sat in a transparent ghostly chair. 'The boy simply does not fit in. Humphrey Bump is a round peg in a square hole.'

'It's hardly my fault the hole is the wrong shape!' I yelled, and Charlie elbowed me in the tummy and told me to shush.

'Take, for instance, the brass-band incident,' the Ghost Headmaster went on. 'I'd arranged for a marching band to parade by the school gates. All went well, until Humphrey here bumped the conductor, and the conductor got his head stuck in the tuba and tumbled into the percussion section, and bounced off the big bass drum, and ended up up-ended in a hedge.'

'Bumping is fun,' I said, and I bumped
the Ghost Headmaster, knocking him off his
ghostly chair.

'You oaf!' the Ghost Headmaster cried,
wisping to his phantom feet. 'Get that boy out
of my school at once.'

4
Plums

That afternoon, I heard the clack-clack-clack of the clicky-clacky typewriter, so I peered into the study, and there was Wither typing up his poems, and Agatha dialling a number on the telephone, and Pamela, Charlie and Tabitha floating by the window.

'Wither,' Charlie said, 'leave it to Agatha. By the time the post-phantom delivers the letter to the other ghost school and the ghostly head teacher types a reply, Humphrey will be old enough for university.'

Wither wasn't typing up his poems as I'd thought. He was typing a letter to another ghost school!

'Don't be mean,' Wither said as he typed with one bony finger. 'The typewritten word carries a certain—'

'Let Wither waste his time if he likes,' Tabitha

said. 'Agatha, have you finished dialling that number yet?'

'My hair keeps blowing into my eyes,' Agatha said, 'and I dial a wrong digit and have to start all over again.'

Agatha Draught is the sort of ghosty who blows an eerie breeze wherever she floats. She's also dead posh.

'There!' Agatha said as she finally finished dialling.

'Put this in your mouth,' Pamela said, and she popped a purple plum between Agatha's lips.

'What is it?' Agatha said, sounding posher than ever.

'A plum,' Pamela said, 'to make your voice plummy.'

'Agatha's voice is plummy enough as it is,' Charlie said, adjusting his tie.

Tabitha and the other grown-up ghosties gathered round to listen as Agatha talked into the mouthpiece. 'We were wondering if you had room for our boy. Humphrey is the name. Humphrey Bump.' Agatha raised an eyebrow at this point, and plonked the telephone receiver back into its cradle.

'What happened?' Tabitha asked.

'The rotter hung up on me,' Agatha said.

Agatha telephoned several other ghost schools, but whenever she mentioned my last name, they hung up.

When Tabitha announced that there were no ghost schools left to call, I bounced through the door and bumped every ghosty in that study – no fibbing!

'Calm down, Humphrey,' Charlie said, straightening his trilby.

'Hooray!' I yelled. 'I won't have to go to Ghost School ever again.'

'I'm afraid Humphrey is right,' Tabitha said. Just as I was about to bounce off to the garden and bump the ghostly gardener into a prickly hedge, Tabitha added, 'There is only one thing for it. Humphrey will have to go to Still-Alive School, with the still-alive children.'

Wither tugged the smudged letter from the clicky-clacky typewriter and crumpled it into a ball. 'But, Agatha, the still-alive children are meanies.'

'It's a mean world,' Agatha said, plucking the plum from between her lips. 'And it's even meaner to those who do not possess a proper education.'

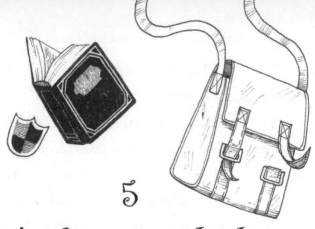

5

Badge, Satchel and Books

I spent the next few days stuffing my mouth with pies, sausages, pizza, pies and cake. If I make myself fat, I thought, my uniform won't fit and I won't have to go to Still-Alive School.

'Almost done,' Agatha said early on Monday morning. Me and the grown-up ghosties were floating about in the lounge, watching her sew a new badge onto my ghostly blazer. 'There,'

Agatha said, and she held up the blazer for all to see.

'Where did you find a ghost Still-Alive School badge?' I asked her, licking my lollipop.

'It's rather a sad tale,' Agatha said, almost in a whisper. 'One of the still-alive pupils climbed into the lion cage at the zoo. The lion ate him in one gulp. When he turned into a ghost, Charlie pinched the ghostly badge from his ghostly blazer.'

'I didn't pinch it,' Charlie said. 'I swapped it for a tub of raspberry-ripple I-scream.'

'Fancy being eaten by a lion,' said Pamela Fraidy. 'The very thought gives me the shivers.'

'Serves the boy right,' Wither said. 'This boy had a nasty habit of bopping felines on the head with a rolled-up comic. Kittens to begin with, then tabby cats and alley cats—'

'I guess he got greedy,' Agatha said. 'Now, try this on.'

'Thank you, Aunty Aggie,' I said. 'I can't wait to start my new school,' I added with a crafty smile.

I slipped my arms into the sleeves, then pulled the blazer at the front, but the buttons wouldn't reach the buttonholes, not even nearly.

'Humphrey,' Charlie said, wisping out from the lampshade, 'you've put on weight.'

'What a pity,' I said, tugging the blazer from my arms. 'I'll just have to stay at home and read comics.'

'You will do no such thing,' Agatha said.

'This explains why he's been eating so much,' Tabitha said.

'Humphrey, you should be ashamed of yourself.'

'You will have to go to Still-Alive School whether the blazer fits or not,' Agatha said.

'But the still-alive children will laugh at me,' I blubbed. 'They'll call me Small-Blazer and poke me with a stick.'

After breakfast, I found Wither and Tabitha in the hall.

'Humphrey,' Tabitha said, 'are you sure you don't want one of us to float to school with you?'

'No, it's fine,' I said as I tied my tie. 'I know the way.'

'Here's your satchel,' Wither said, passing me the horrible leather bag. 'I've packed the complete works of Shakespeare, Wordsworth and Dickens. Oh, I also included a few of my own writings, typed in double spacing on the clicky-clacky typewriter.'

'He'll never read all that,' Tabitha said.

She opened the front door using her poltergeist powers, and I floated out into the late-summer sun.

The moment Tabitha closed the door, I floated behind the hedge, dragging the phantom satchel. A second later, the door opened with an eerie creak.

'Can you see him?' I heard Tabitha ask.

'No, I can't,' Wither replied. 'He's so excited to meet his new friends, he'll be bouncing up that road without a care in the world.'

'I doubt he'll bounce far with all those heavy books,' Tabitha said, and the door slammed closed.

I really did want to float to Still-Alive School, honest I did, but the thought of all those new faces—

Oh, and I'd forgotten my pencil case, and—

Anyway, my tummy told me it was time

for an early lunch, so I hid the satchel in the stinging nettles and floated over the house and in through the larder window.

I had barely eaten half a sponge cake when in floated Charlie Vapour.

'Um,' I said, wiping icing from my mouth. 'There was an earthquake, so the Still-Alive Headmaster sent us home, and the earthquake shook the shelf and the cake toppled into my mouth and—'

'Humphrey,' Charlie said as he toyed with his trilby, 'you're a big, cake-eating fibber. Wipe your mouth. I'm wisping you to Still-Alive School myself.'

Charlie's Polite Advice

Still-Alive School wasn't like our old grey Ghost School. The building was built from red bricks and had a roof as flat and boring as a maths book.

When we arrived, the still-alive children screamed at us and ran into the classrooms. The sun shone so brightly on the windows that I couldn't see in, but I knew the children were inside.

'I think I'll just float about in the playground,' I said, dragging my satchel over the railing.

'If all you do is waft about on your own,' Charlie said, 'you might as well have stayed in your room.'

I smiled when Charlie said this. 'If we leave now,' I said, 'we can be home in a float, a wisp and a flit.'

'That's not what I meant. School is about more than just the written word, Humphrey.'

'What is it about, then?'

Charlie held his hat to his chest and frowned in thought. 'School is about making girls blush behind the bike shed, and beating the school bully at conkers. At least, that's how I remember it from when I was a boy.'

'I don't want to do those things,' I said as Charlie peered at me through the railings.

'Look,' Charlie said, pointing. 'There's

another boy who's arrived late. If you float over and say hello, you might make a new friend.'

'He won't like me,' I said. 'I'm a ghost.'

'I'll hold your satchel. Off you float.'

I waited until the boy opened the door to the school building, then wisped across the playground and bumped him so hard he landed on the concrete in a heap – no fibbing!

The boy scrambled to his feet and ran out through the school gates in tears.

'Humphrey!' Charlie yelled. 'Why did you bump the poor lad?'

'To teach him a lesson for making fun of me.'

'But he didn't make fun of you,' Charlie said.

'He would have, if I hadn't bumped him.'

Charlie dragged the satchel across the playground towards me. 'If you want to get along in this world, you must learn to be polite. All it takes is a smile and a doff of the hat—'

'I don't wear a hat.'

'Bump this door open,' Charlie said, 'and I'll show you what I mean.'

Charlie left the satchel of books on the doorstep and led me along a corridor lined with shiny red doors. From behind one of the doors, we could hear a lady teacher yawning on about sums.

'Watch,' Charlie said with a wink, 'and learn.'

'Learning is what I'm here for,' I said with a gulp.

Charlie held his trilby to his chest – the polite thing to do – and passed through the wall and into the classroom.

'Forgive me for interrupting,' I heard him say, but before he could finish, the teacher

shrieked at the top of her lungs and the
still-alive children made the most frightful
row.

'Not quite the reaction I expected,' Charlie
said, passing back.

I tugged a chocolate biscuit from my trouser
pocket and took a bite. 'You see? The still-alive
children are meanies, just like
Wither said.'

7

Wither's Abysmal Poetry

That evening, Tabitha and Charlie had a
grown-up talk in the study. I wisped into the
clicky-clacky typewriter where I could watch
and listen in secret.

'Humphrey used to be so popular,' Tabitha
said, 'but then he started bumping.'

'He's always bumped,' Charlie said,
adjusting his trilby, 'ever since he was still alive.'

'I doubt he bumped as much as he does now, Charlie.'

'I've tried talking to the boy,' Charlie said, 'but I can't get through to him.'

At that moment Wither wisped in. 'I have it!' he cried, wriggling his candlestick fingers.

'Calm down, Wither,' Tabitha said. 'Take a deep breath and tell us your idea.'

Wither took a deep breath, but when he spoke he sounded more excited than ever. 'It is as easy as algebra. If we do the still-alive pupils a good deed, they will look upon us ghosties with kindness and embrace Master Bump as a friend.'

'What do you have in mind?' Charlie said.

'If there is one thing children love,' Wither said with a smile, 'it is vegetables. And if there is one other thing children love, it is poetry.'

Charlie adjusted his tie. 'Oh, I don't know about that.'

'Tell us your plan,' said Tabitha, sounding dead kind.

'I will compose a vegetable-themed poem,' Wither announced in his warbly poetry voice, 'and recite it to the children during their English lesson.'

A moment later, Wither's fingers floated above the keys, so I wisped out of the clicky-clacky typewriter. I wanted to stay as far away from Wither's poetry as possible.

'Humphrey!' Tabitha said. 'You've been listening all this time.'

'Please don't let Wither write a poem about vegetables,' I said, trying not to blub. 'I hate vegetables, and Wither's poems are drivel.'

'Don't be mean,' said Wither.

'If Wither reads his poems at the school,' I said, 'the still-alive children will hate us ghosties more than ever.'

'Dear boy,' Wither said, 'you lack faith.'

He fed a sheet of paper into the clicky-clacky typewriter and began to type.

During the night, I could hear the click-clack of keys, and Wither wailing poetically into the darkness. 'Oh, the muse!' he wailed. 'Oh, the muse!'

When I floated into the study after breakfast, Wither lay slumped over the clicky-clacky typewriter. Agatha and Tabitha were trying to shake him awake.

'I barely slept a wink,' I said with a yawn.

'Wither,' Tabitha said, 'it's time to float to Still-Alive School and recite the poem.'

'I'm too tired to recite the, um, carrot,' Wither mumbled, prising his eyes open with his bony fingers.

'But, Wither,' Agatha said, 'you've been working on that poem all night. It would be a shame not to recite it.'

'Wake me when I'm broccoli,' Wither said,

and his haunted head flopped against the keys.

'Why did the poem take so long to write?' Tabitha asked Wither, shaking his left shoulder. 'Is it a particularly good poem?'

'It is more that it's a particularly long poem,' Wither yawned, scooping up a pile of papers. 'A twelve-thousand-page poetic epic. Come along, Humphrey. We have young minds to nurture.'

The float to school took forever. Wither kept nodding off, and every few seconds a page would sail away on the warm summer breeze and Tabitha would chase after it.

'He's fading,' I whispered to

Tabitha as the three of us wafted by the school gates.

'Wither,' Tabitha said, 'you're so tired you've turned transparent.'

'All ghosties are transparent,' Wither yawned.

'Not as transparent as that,' Tabitha said, 'and not all over. You're so see-through you're barely visible. Why not float off home and get some sleep?'

Wither shrugged, and watched lazily as

twelve thousand sheets of paper blew across the playground. 'I will have to recite my masterpiece from memory.'

The three of us flitted around the school building until we found a classroom with an open window. Inside, we could hear a lady teacher rattling on about verbs and nouns.

Wither was so tired now we could barely see him at all.

'I'll just write the poem on the whiteboard, then float off home to bed,' Wither yawned, and he wisped into the classroom.

'I doubt they'll have enough ink,' Tabitha giggled.

Tabitha and me wisped into a plant pot on the window sill and waited.

A moment later a pen lifted from the teacher's desk and scrawled the words ODE TO VEGETABLES on the whiteboard.

The teacher fainted, and the still-alive children leapt from their seats and screamed.

'At least wait until I've written the first line,' Wither's voice said, 'before you pass judgement.'

But the still-alive children were already scrambling over their desks and barging out through the classroom door.

8
Agatha's Helpful Breeze

Tabitha said I could spend the rest of the week at home, reading comics. Well, literature really, but I'd torn up my comics and hidden the pieces between the pages of Wither's books.

The comics didn't make much sense jumbled up like that, but they still made more sense than Dickens.

On Saturday, me, Tabitha, Agatha and Wither floated down to the village park.

'The still-alive children will yell mean names and run away,' I said.

'I doubt they'll be able to see us in this bright sunlight,' Agatha said.

The park was dead busy, with families sat on tartan blankets scoffing sandwiches from paper plates, and dogs chasing sticks, and nannies pushing baby still-alives in prams.

'Look at the children on the hill there,' Wither said, pointing. 'They're trying to fly kites, but there's no wind.'

'We can't have that,' Tabitha said. 'Aggie, you could create a breeze using your skills.'

'Tabitha, dearest,' Agatha said, clutching her pearls, 'with my limited abilities, I doubt I could blow the froth from a mug of coffee.'

'Modesty has its place, dear Aggie,' Wither said, 'but the boy here needs an education.'

All ghostly eyes turned to me.

'Wither,' Agatha said, 'what could you possibly mean?'

'The kite problem is nothing more than an opportunity stood upon its head.'

'What are you talking about?' Tabitha said.

'It is as simple as sums,' Wither said, and he waved his fingers like sticks of Frighten rock. 'What if Agatha were to rustle up a force-ten gale as Tabitha suggests? The still-alive children will adore us ghosties after that, the Bump boy included.'

'Me? A force-ten gale?' Agatha said with a blustery laugh. 'I can barely blow the seeds from a dandelion.'

'Rubbish,' Tabitha said. 'We've all seen the way you dry Wither's long johns.'

Wither folded his coat hanger arms. 'Agatha, the educational diet of a hungry mind is at stake.'

'My mind is the only part of me that isn't hungry,' I said. 'Anyway, what's the point in helping the still-alives? They'll only be mean to me.'

'No one is mean in the park on a Saturday,' Wither said. 'Not even the still-alive children are mean in the park on a Saturday.'

'Well, I think the plan is rotten,' I said as the four of us floated up the hillside. 'I wouldn't mind flying a kite though.'

Agatha raised a posh eyebrow at a girl holding a floppy kite. 'Now, there's a young lady who'd appreciate a gust or two.'

'Off you float then,' Tabitha said.

For a moment Agatha looked ready to flit into action, but then she shrugged, rolled her eyes, rattled her pearls and said, 'I can't do it with you three watching.'

'We'll turn the other way,' Wither said, and we did.

But then we turned back.

The three of us watched as Agatha wisped around the girl in a circle, once, twice, again and again and again, faster and faster, until the kite broke free of the girl's arms and lifted into the air.

'Good old Aggie!' Tabitha cried, clapping her hands.

'But she's doing it wrong,' I said. 'Look.'

Tabitha yelled at Agatha to stop, but it was too late. The kite began to spin, and the string twisted this way and that and coiled around the girl like a snake.

'Help!' the girl cried as her mother and father ran to the rescue. 'Help!'

'Stand still,' the father called, but the girl lost her balance and rolled off down the hill.

'Never mind,' Tabitha said when Agatha floated back. 'Have another go.' She squinted into the sun and pointed towards the very top of the hill. 'What about that boy there?'

The four of us floated up the hillside to where a tiny boy raced through the long grass, an orange kite held high above his head.

'A bit less round-and-round,' Agatha said to herself, 'and a lot more up-and-up.'

'We'll turn the other way,' I said, and we did. But then we turned back.

'There she blows!' Tabitha said. 'Good old Aggie.'

The three of us watched open-mouthed as the orange kite soared high into the bright blue sky.

'Isn't Agatha wisping a bit fast?' I said.

'You're right,' Wither said. 'The poor still-alive is struggling to keep up.'

Tabitha gasped as the boy's trainers lifted from the ground. Up and up he went, gripping the wooden reel with his fingers.

'The kite is carrying him away,' I said. 'Why doesn't he let go?'

'It's too late for that,' Wither said. 'If he hits the ground from that height, he'll turn into one of us.'

The other still-alives stopped scoffing sandwiches and pushing prams and throwing sticks for dogs, and ran after the terrified, tiny boy. Perhaps they thought they'd be able to catch him if he let go of the reel.

'Help!' the boy cried. 'Help! Help!'

'We have to get him down!' one of the still-alives yelled.

'He'll bump his head on an aeroplane!' yelled another.

'And what if he's pecked by birds!' yelled another.

Whenever the boy bobbed beneath the clouds, the still-alives ran towards him, but then he'd disappear out of sight and reappear

somewhere else, and the still-alives would have to run in a different direction.

Then a gust of wind sent the boy sailing off to the east, and the still-alives ran out through the park gates, dogs yapping at their heels.

We floated around for a bit, then Agatha said, 'We might as well enjoy ourselves, while we're here.' And she wisped off over the hill.

'Where's she gone?' I said, and Wither and Tabitha shrugged.

When Agatha floated back a minute later, she held four ghostly raspberry-ripple I-screams.

'Good old Aggie,' Tabitha said, and we gave our I-screams a joyful lick.

As we floated home through the village later that afternoon, we came across a crowd of still-alives gathered on the pavement by the church.

'Today must be Sunday,' Wither said.

'It can't be,' Tabitha said. 'It was Saturday when we left the house.'

We floated closer. The still-alives were gawping at a boy bound to the church spire, an orange kite dangling from his ankle.

Several newspaper reporters were taking photographs and scrawling in their notepads. A policeman propped a ladder against the church wall, but it barely reached the roof.

Two minutes later, the crowd parted as a fire engine roared down the street, sounding its siren.

'What a brave little boy,' Agatha said, and we wisped off home.

9
Humphrey's
New Friend

Whatever the grown-up ghosties did, nothing seemed to help.

On Monday I floated to Still-Alive School alone. When I peered through the railings I saw two still-alive boys teasing a girl.

'Fatty-Fatty Pigtails!' the boys yelled. 'Fatty-Fatty Pigtails!'

'I'm not fat,' the girl said, rubbing her

round tummy. 'And these aren't pigtails. They're plaits.'

She started to blub, and the boys laughed.

I felt a funny feeling in my tummy. Not the funny feeling I get when I've eaten candyfloss on toast. No, this was an angry feeling.

I wisped over the railing and bumped the two boys to the ground.

The girl screamed.

'I'm sorry,' I said. 'I didn't mean to scare you.'

The girl dried her eyes and peered at me through her glasses. 'You rescued me.'

'Yes,' I said.

'I'm ever so grateful. But you're – you're see-through, and you float.'

'I'm a ghost,' I said, 'a real live ghost.' I pinched myself, then added, 'Well, a real dead ghost.'

'You're not like the ghosts in films. You have a friendly face.'

'Oh, I'm frightfully friendly,' I said, and I wriggled my transparent bits.

The girl tugged her plaits. 'I have to go now, or I'll be in trouble.'

'All right,' I said. 'My name is Humphrey, by the way. Humphrey Bump.'

'I can see why they call you Bump,' the girl said, glancing at the two bruised boys. 'My name is Amelia. I have to run now, or I'll be late for maths.'

When I arrived home I found the girl ghosties baking cakes in the kitchen. Wither floated above the stove reading a spooky cookery book.

'You look happy,' Tabitha said.

'I had a good day at Still-Alive School,' I said, dumping my satchel on the kitchen table.

'Rather a short good day,' Wither said,

checking the time on his pocket watch. 'School begins at nine o'clock sharp. It is barely a minute after ten.'

'At least he went,' Agatha said. 'Humphrey, tell us what happened.'

'I made friends with a still-alive girl,' I said, grabbing a handful of cherries.

Wither frowned. 'But the still-alive children are meanies.'

'Not once you get to know them.'

'You should float to school again this afternoon,' Tabitha said, 'before your new friend forgets who you are.'

'I'll do that,' I said, and I did.

The trouble was, when I arrived at Still-Alive School there were so many children in the playground I thought I'd never find her.

'Amelia?' I yelled. 'Is anyone friends with Amelia?'

Wherever I floated, children yelled mean things and ran away.

I'd almost given up when a familiar voice called out from a group of girl still-alives. I smiled a smile as big as a slice of raspberry pie. 'Amelia!'

'Humphrey,' Amelia said, glancing round at her fleeing friends, 'I can't be friends with you. I'm sorry.'

'Oh,' I said, trying not to blub. 'Well, I just thought you might like to share this chocolate bar. It's

ghost chocolate, so you won't be able to eat it,
but—'

'This is why we can't be friends,' Amelia
said. 'You're a ghost, and I'm still alive.'

'I wish I was still alive too,' I said, and I
wisped off.

10
Eggs, Bacon and Porridge

'I may be round,' I muttered as I rolled out of bed the next morning, 'but I'm no quitter.'

Charlie passed his head through the bedroom door. 'Talking to yourself, Humphrey Bump?'

'Knock before you pass through,' I said. 'It's the polite thing to do, and I might be getting dressed.'

'I tried knocking,' Charlie said, 'but it's rather a thin door and my knuckles passed through the wood.'

At breakfast, the grown-up ghosties asked me about my new friend.

'Is she pretty?' Charlie said, prising the lid from the marmalade jar.

Wither cracked the shell of a boiled egg. 'Charlie, for one so polite, you possess frightfully poor manners.'

'Is she charming?' Pamela asked as she buttered the ghostly toast.

'Oh, and is she a swot?' Agatha said. 'I mean, is she clever?'

I didn't say anything.

'At least tell us your new girlfriend's name,' Agatha said, and she blew the steam from her porridge.

'Her name is Amelia,' I mumbled into my bacon and eggs, 'but she isn't my—'

'Just good friends,' Tabitha said with a wink.

'That wasn't what I meant. When I talked to Amelia in the playground yesterday afternoon, she said she can't be friends with a ghosty.'

'Oh, the meanness!' cried Wither, and he dunked a soldier into his egg yolk.

'Let's face it,' Charlie said, 'Still-Alive School just isn't ready for a phantom pupil.'

The grown-up ghosties peered at me over their plates and bowls, and I felt like wisping off to my room and hiding under the bed.

Then Charlie lifted his hat from the table, flicked a crumb from the brim, and placed the hat on his head. 'Except that Humphrey isn't a quitter. Isn't that right, Humphrey?'

I thought back to how brave I'd felt earlier that morning, when I rolled out of bed. 'It's time I packed my satchel,' I said, and I floated out to the hall.

'Good on you, Humphrey,' Tabitha said.

'What about your breakfast?' Charlie called.

'I want to arrive early,' I called back, 'while there aren't too many still-alives about.'

When I wisped down the ornate staircase, my school tie wafting behind me, I found Tabitha, Charlie, Wither, Agatha and Pamela floating by the front door.

'We thought we'd come with you,' Agatha said. 'If we put our haunted heads together—'

Tabitha clapped her hands, and the front door creaked open.

'I need to solve this problem for myself,' I said as the six of us floated out of the house.

'How mean,' said Wither, and he pursed his lips.

When I looked round, the grown-up ghosties had gone.

Bumping Lessons

As I floated across the empty playground, past the prickly bushes decorated with crisp packets and flowers, an idea struck.

My idea was that I'd wisp into one of the classrooms, find a seat at the back, and float above it doing sums. By the time the lesson started, the still-alives would be used to my ghostly presence, and they wouldn't be mean to me.

That's what it's called when there's a ghost

in the room. A ghostly presence. Wither told me that, and Wither is a poet.

I found a classroom with an open window and floated in.

When I opened my spooky satchel, five frightfully friendly ghosties wisped out.

'We're here to help you make friends,' Agatha said.

'It was my idea,' Charlie said, and he held his hat to his chest.

'Charlie, don't boast,' Agatha said. 'It's hardly the polite thing to do.'

'I did doff my trilby, Agatha.'

'Anyway,' Pamela said, hiding her eyes, 'it was my idea, not Charlie Vapour's.'

Wither folded his bony arms. 'But I was the first ghosty to wisp into Humphrey's satchel.'

'I'm sure we all thought of it together,' Tabitha said.

'Well,' I said, 'I don't care who thought of it. The idea stinks.'

The school bell buzzed, and Pamela screamed.

'What a frightful noise,' Agatha said, and she plugged her ears with her fingers.

'It's time for lessons to start,' I said, 'and you grown-up ghosties have ruined everything.'

'But we came to help,' Tabitha said.

'I don't need your help. I just want the still-alive children to like me. If they see you lot, they'll hate me more than ever.'

The classroom door opened, and a still-alive girl walked in. When she saw six frightfully friendly ghosties, she screamed and ran off down the corridor.

'Told you,' I said, and I blew a raspberry.

Wither held a bony finger to his lips. 'Shh! Listen!'

We listened.

'Fatty-Fatty Pigtails! Fatty-Fatty Pigtails!' a voice called.

We turned to the window, and could just make out three figures on the other side of the prickly hedge.

'That's Amelia,' I said. 'Those two boys are bullies.'

'You should bump them,' Charlie said with a wink.

'Amelia will certainly want to be friends if you rescue her from bullies,' Tabitha said.

'I've already tried that.'

'Then bump them again,' said Wither. 'Some bullies need bumping twice.'

'Teach them a lesson!' Charlie yelled as I wisped out through the open window.

As I floated over the prickly hedge, another idea struck. I knew I couldn't protect Amelia forever. Perhaps I could teach her to protect herself.

I wisped into Amelia's left ear and whispered, 'Bump them.'

'Humphrey,' Amelia said, 'is that you?'

'Yes,' I whispered. 'Amelia, you have a round tummy, like me. Put it to good use and bump the bullies into the hedge.'

'I couldn't, Humphrey. I'd get into trouble with the Headmaster.'

Another idea struck, the third I'd had that day. I wisped out of Amelia's left ear, took a deep breath and bumped poor Amelia, sending her bouncing into the two boys, who landed upside down in the prickly hedge.

Inside the classroom, the five grown-up ghosties cheered.

'Humphrey,' Amelia said, brushing gravel from her knees, 'we bumped the bullies.'

'Next time you're bullied, you'll know what to do,' I said, and I floated off, leaving Amelia smiling proudly.

12
The Still-Alive Headmaster

'I'm glad we decided to be friends,' Amelia said that afternoon. 'School playtimes can be fun now.'

We sat together on a bench at the edge of the playground. Well, Amelia sat, and I floated.

'I can eat my ordinary crisps,' Amelia said as she crunched, 'and you can eat your ghost crisps, and—'

'But, Amelia, you're crying.'

'School is horrid,' Amelia said, and she blew her nose on her left plait.

'It needn't be, now that we're friends.'

Amelia shook her head. 'There will always be bullying in this world, Humphrey, no matter who you're friends with.'

'Bump them, like how I taught you.'

'There are some bullies who just can't be bumped.'

'I'm not afraid of any bully,' I said, and I munched another creepy crisp.

Amelia frowned, then looked at me and said, 'You'd be afraid of this bully.'

'Why? Who is he?'

'The Headmaster.'

I laughed, spilling crisps down my blazer. 'I bumped the Ghost Headmaster at Ghost School. No one bullies Humphrey Bump.'

'Didn't you get into trouble?'

'He'd already expelled me,' I explained. 'That's why I'm here, at Still-Alive School.'

'Humphrey, I can't get expelled. I'm top of the class in science. I plan to go to university.'

'Then you'd better stay out of his way,' I said, opening another bag of crisps.

'I can't,' Amelia said, and she began to cry again. 'I have to see the Headmaster today after school.'

'But why?'

Amelia sniffed into her crisp packet, and said, 'For bumping bullies.'

At last bell, I floated in through the window of the Still-Alive Headmaster's office and wisped behind the potted plant.

As I peered out between the dusty green leaves, I heard a faint phantom blub.

'Wither,' I whispered, 'is that you?'

'I'm hiding in the hem of the curtain,' Wither blubbed. 'I wisped in, and now I can't wisp out.'

'What do you mean, you can't wisp out?'

'The Still-Alive Headmaster is mean,' Wither blubbed.

'You don't get to be a headmaster without being mean, Wither.'

'This headmaster is so mean he makes other headmasters seem scarcely mean at all.'

'But, Wither, why did you float into the Still-Alive Headmaster's office in the first place?'

'I wanted to see how mean he was,' Wither said, and he blubbed.

The office door opened, and a girl walked in.

'Humphrey,' Wither sniffed, 'that girl looks familiar.'

'She's my still-alive friend, Amelia,' I whispered. 'Amelia has been sent to the Headmaster for bumping bullies into the hedge.'

'That's triple mean,' Wither blubbed. 'The bullies were mean to Amelia, then Amelia was mean to the bullies, and now the Still-Alive Headmaster—'

'Keep quiet,' I whispered. 'I want to hear what he says.'

From my hiding place behind the leaves of the potted plant, I could just make out the Still-Alive Headmaster sat at his desk, and Amelia nervously biting her fingernails.

'Well?' the Still-Alive Headmaster yelled. 'What do you have to say for yourself, child?'

'I'm sorry, sir,' Amelia said. 'Um, it won't happen again, and—'

'Not good enough, child!' the Headmaster yelled, his face the colour of beetroot.

Amelia backed away as the Still-Alive Headmaster stood from his chair and leant towards her across the desk, jabbing the air with a spiny finger.

'Lines!' the Still-Alive Headmaster yelled. 'Ten thousand, in your neatest handwriting.

Fifty hours litter duty. And two hours detention each day for a month.'

'Oh, the meanness!' Wither blubbed, and he wisped up from the hem of the curtain and floated out through the office window.

For a moment the Still-Alive Headmaster looked almost afraid. 'What in heaven's name was that?'

'A friend of a friend,' Amelia said, and she walked out of the Headmaster's office with a smile.

13

Who's Afraid of Humphrey Bump?

'Haven't you noticed,' Amelia whispered on Wednesday afternoon, 'how unhappy everyone is?'

'I'm sure they'd rather be out riding their bicycles in the sun,' I said, peering out from Amelia's satchel. 'Anything other than opening their maths books.'

'That's not what I meant.' Amelia

z z Z Z z z z z

sat at her desk and lowered the satchel to the floor. 'School days are supposed to be the best days of your life. Ever since this new headmaster arrived last term, I've not seen one cheerful face.'

I broke a chunk from a ghostly chocolate bar and popped it into my mouth.

'And look at how tired everyone is, Humphrey.'

I peered out of the satchel and glanced around the classroom. Two of the boys had their heads in their arms. One girl was snoring loudly. 'They stayed up late watching cartoons, I guess.'

'Cartoons? Humphrey, after a day of lessons, followed by five hours of homework, I doubt they can keep their eyes open.'

'Five hours of homework?'

'Headmaster's rules,' Amelia whispered.

The room fell silent as the Still-Alive

Headmaster strode in on his long, mean legs. He glanced around the classroom, then pointed at a boy in the front row. 'You, child, where is the teacher?'

'You – you fired her, sir,' the boy stammered.

'Raise your hand when you speak, child,' the Headmaster yelled, and the boy raised his hand. 'You're expelled. Gather your pencils, child, and get out.'

'You can't expel a boy for forgetting to raise his hand,' I whispered.

'We're lucky he's in a good mood,' Amelia whispered back, 'or he'd have expelled the entire class.'

'He can't do that!'

'It's happened before, Humphrey. I told you the headmaster was a bully.'

'Well, it's got to stop,' I said.

'Humphrey,' Amelia gasped, 'what are you going to do?'

'You've heard of things that go bump in the night? Well, I'm going to go bump in the daytime, right here in this maths room.'

'You'll get yourself into trouble.'

I loosened my school tie. 'What can he do, expel me?'

'Just be careful, Humphrey.'

'He's the one who should be careful,' I said, and I wisped out from Amelia's satchel. The still-alive children screamed and ran out of the classroom, and the Still-Alive Headmaster backed into the corner. I took a deep breath and gave the Still-Alive Headmaster the bumpiest bump I'd ever bumped.

'Ghostly child,' the Headmaster said, straightening his hairpiece, 'surely you can bump me better than that?'

'How do you mean?'

'Must try harder,' the Still-Alive Headmaster said, and he walked out of the classroom.

'But that was my best-ever bump,' I said, tugging a jam doughnut from my blazer pocket. I'd intended to bump him again, but somehow I'd lost heart.

'Perhaps you don't need to bump him,' Amelia said from the doorway. 'You're a ghost, Humphrey. Most people find ghosts terrifying.'

'I'd forgotten about that,' I said, and I wisped off down the corridor, wriggling my transparent bits and pulling a mean face.

The Still-Alive Headmaster just stood there shaking his head – pitifully, I think.

'I'm a ghost,' I said. 'Aren't you afraid?'

'Not in the least,' the Still-Alive Headmaster said, and he walked off.

14

Humphrey's Speech

Thursday morning, as I floated across the field to Still-Alive School, I bumped into Wither.

'I thought you'd stopped all that bumping nonsense,' Wither said.

'Sorry.'

I told Wither about what had happened with the Still-Alive Headmaster in the maths room.

'Some still-alives are afraid of ghosties,' I said, 'but not this still-alive. I wriggled my transparent bits and he didn't bat an eyelid.'

Wither rubbed his chin. 'And you bumped him, you say?'

'Left, right and centre,' I said, picking an apple from a nearby apple tree.

'He must be afraid of something. Every still-alive is afraid of something.'

'Well,' I said, 'he did look afraid when you wisped out from his curtains. Only for a moment, then he sort of pulled himself together.'

'Hmm,' Wither said. 'It seems to me that this mean-spirited still-alive is indeed afraid of ghosties, but only a bit.'

'What are you getting at?' I said, crunching the rosy apple.

'It's like this. Let's say I've just penned a quite-good poem. If I wish to lift the poem to greatness, I simply write a further two hundred verses.'

'But that makes the poem worse,' I said.

'Your poetry is drivel. The less of it there is, the better.'

Wither didn't seem to hear. I think he was lost in a poetic reverie or something.

I tossed the half-eaten apple into a hedge. 'Wither, I know you're trying to help—'

'Allow me to finish,' Wither said. 'If this headmaster is afraid of one ghosty a bit, he will be afraid of a lot of ghosties a lot.'

I thought about this for a moment, then said, 'That actually makes sense.'

'Let's see.' Wither held up his knitting-needle fingers and began to count. 'There's myself, you and I – that's three. And the three girl ghosties makes six. And then there's Charlie. And Humphrey – that's you – which makes eight—'

'Shh,' I said. 'Listen.'

Wither cupped his ear with his hand. 'But, Humphrey, you're not saying anything.'

'Not to me. To, um, everything else.'

We listened.

Wither said, 'I can't hear anything. Well, only the ghost children at Ghost School across the field there, but—'

'Wait here,' I said, and I flitted across the field and over the high grey wall and into the Ghost School playground.

After a quick float around, I spotted Samuel Spook floating by the bike shed.

We used to be good friends, but when I wafted across the playground towards him he turned up his nose.

'Samuel,' I said, 'I need your help. There's this headmaster at Still-Alive School, and—'

'I can't hear you,' Samuel said, and he poked his fingers into his ears.

'But, Samuel, we're friends.'

'After you bumped me into the sausage trolley in the canteen?'

'I'd forgotten about that.'

'Fight your own battles,' Samuel said, and he floated off.

Just as I felt ready to give up and wisp back to Wither, I spotted the terrifying twins, Phil and Fay Phantom.

When I floated over, Fay folded her arms, and Phil looked through his shoes.

'I need your help,' I said. 'There's this headmaster—'

'You've got a nerve,' Phil said.

'You bumped me into the swimming pool,' Fay said, and she tossed her hair.

'Only in fun, Fay.'

'And you bumped me down the stairs,' Phil said. 'If I wasn't dead, I might've been hurt.'

'I can explain.'

'Don't bother,' the twins said together, and off they wisped.

I floated, slowly, back over the high grey wall and across the field to where Wither wafted poetically beneath the leaves of a sycamore tree.

'Humphrey, you look like you've found a cupcake and dropped it.'

I explained how the ghost children refused to help, and about how they hated me because I'd bumped them.

'What you must do,' Wither said, 'is return to Ghost School and move the children to tears with a heartfelt speech. The children will flock to your cause like moths to a flame.'

'I'm no good with words, Wither.'

'I'll wisp back to the house,' Wither said,

chewing a wasp, 'and write a speech on the clicky-clacky typewriter.'

'If you don't mind, I'd rather make it up as I go along.'

Together we floated across the field, higher this time, so high that the sheep and trees and the Ghost School building looked like toys.

I floated down, waving my arms above my head. The children gathered round to hear what I had to say.

'I'm sorry for bumping you. I just wanted to have fun, that's all.'

'Boo!' the children booed. 'Boo! Boo!'

'Please listen,' I said. 'There's this headmaster at Still-Alive School, and he's a bully, and, um—'

'Boo! Boo!'

'Look,' I said, 'if you don't help me, I won't have a school to go to, and I'll have to study at home with Wither.'

'The boring old Victorian poet?' Phil Phantom said.

'That's what you get for bumping us,' Samuel Spook said.

I shrugged, bit into a jam doughnut and wisped off.

15

Crime and Punishment

I found Amelia in the corridor, outside the Still-Alive Headmaster's office.

'Humphrey,' Amelia said, 'something terrible has happened.'

'What?'

'The Headmaster heard the bullies calling me names. He's given them lines. One million each, in their best handwriting.'

I shrugged.

'It's wrong,' Amelia said. 'The punishment should fit the crime, don't you think?'

We peered into the office. The Still-Alive Headmaster was standing between the two boys and the open door.

'We can't write a million lines,' one of the bullies said.

The Still-Alive Headmaster folded his arms. 'You're not leaving my office until you do.'

'We've got to get them out of there,' I whispered.

'Bump him,' Amelia whispered back.

'I don't think I can,' I groaned, holding my tummy. 'I've just eaten twelve jam doughnuts.'

'If you don't bump him,' Amelia whispered, 'I will.'

'You'll get expelled, and you won't be able to go to university.' I reached out to stop her but my hand passed right through. When I feel queasy, I tend to fade a bit.

Amelia took a deep breath and bumped the Headmaster's bottom.

The two boys exchanged looks. 'It's Fatty-Fatty Pigtails,' one of them said as they slipped past the Still-Alive Headmaster.

'Um, I don't think we should call her that,' the other boy said. 'That girl just saved our bacon.'

'You are both expelled!' the Headmaster yelled, but the boys ran off up the corridor and out into the playground.

We followed the Still-Alive Headmaster as he strode through the school grounds, pointing at still-alive children with a long, mean finger.

'Expelled!' he yelled. 'Expelled, expelled, expelled!'

Amelia gasped.

'That's right,' he said, fixing his eyes on Amelia. 'I am expelling every pupil in this school.'

16

The Headmaster's Wife

On Friday morning a crowd of still-alive children gathered at the school gates. I didn't want them to see me, so I flitted round to the back of the school and wisped over the fence.

'I'm glad you're here, Humphrey,' Amelia said when we met in the back playground. 'Something big is happening, and I need your help.'

'I didn't think anyone would be here,' I said. 'I thought you'd all been expelled.'

'Not yet. The Headmaster has to fill in forms and write to the parents.'

'That Headmaster is so mean,' I said, 'he'll do it, even if it takes him all night,'

Amelia smiled. 'He'll have to get into his office first.'

I followed Amelia to the main entrance. Two boys blocked our path.

'Friend or foe?' one of the boys barked.

The boys wore scout caps pulled down over their eyes. Each had a badge taped to his blazer, just below the left shoulder. SECURITY, the badges read.

'It's me – Amelia. If you pulled your caps up you'd be able to see properly.'

The boys lifted their caps, and I recognised them as the bullies. 'Oh, hello,' they both said together.

'They've been good as gold since I rescued them from the Headmaster,' Amelia told me. 'I've put them in charge of security.'

One of the boys opened the door and gestured for us to step inside.

'Amelia,' I said as I followed her down the corridor, 'what's happening?'

'We've taken over the school. The Headmaster can't expel us if he's not in charge.'

I opened a can of fizzy pop.

'And it's not just here,' Amelia went on. 'Every school in the country has put down their pencils, kicked back their chairs and made a stand.'

'That's not a good idea,' I said. 'When the Headmaster hears of this—'

'He won't be able to do a thing. Look.'

The door to the Headmaster's office had been sealed shut with pink stuff.

'Bubble gum,' Amelia said. She took my haunted hand and said, 'Come on.'

'Where are we going now?'

Amelia led me out into the front playground. The air buzzed with cheers and jeers.

'This has got out of hand,' I said.

'What choice is there?' Amelia said. 'After all, if we let the Headmaster into his office, we'll all be expelled.'

'Where is the Headmaster now?'

We heard the screech of car brakes, and Amelia ran across the playground to the railings. I floated up into the air for a better view.

The Still-Alive Headmaster had parked his car right outside the gates. He opened the driver's door and stepped onto the pavement.

'Headmaster, Headmaster, you're so mean!' the children chanted. 'The meanest headmaster we've ever seen!'

'Children,' the Still-Alive Headmaster said, 'go home, or you will be arrested by the police.'

I flitted down and floated at Amelia's side. 'The police would sooner arrest him than you lot,' I told her.

'I'm not so sure. The Police Chief is the Headmaster's wife.'

The Still-Alive Headmaster tried to walk through the gates, but the still-alive pupils linked arms and jostled about.

Several police cars and police vans pulled up, their lights flashing, their sirens wailing. The police officers leapt out, buttoning their tunics and fastening the straps on their helmets.

'That must be the Headmaster's wife,' Amelia said, pointing at a fierce-looking woman in a peaked cap.

'Children,' the woman yelled through a loudhailer, 'place your hands on your heads. You are all under arrest.'

'You can't arrest us!' the children cried. 'We're children!'

'I'll get my dad onto you,' one boy shouted.

Nothing the still-alive boys and girls could say did any good. The Police Chief blew her whistle, and the police officers grabbed the children by the arms and led them back to the police vehicles.

'We have to do something,' I said, but Amelia just shrugged.

'There's nothing we can do, Humphrey. We can't resist the entire police force.'

'Perhaps I can frighten them,' I said, and I wisped across the road, poked out my tongue and blew a raspberry.

The police officers and the children screamed, but the Still-Alive Headmaster just laughed. 'That,' he yelled, pointing at me with his mean finger, 'is nothing but a trick of the light.'

Amelia stepped out through the gates with her hands on her head. 'It's no use,' she told me. 'We might as well give ourselves up.'

'Never,' I said, and I bumped the Still-Alive Headmaster into his wife.

'There,' I said, winking at Amelia. 'That should shut them up.'

'I doubt it, Humphrey. It's like I said. There are some bullies you just can't bump.'

The Still-Alive Headmaster helped the Police Chief to her feet. 'Spectral child,' he said, 'you can bump my wife and me till the cows come home. We're not going to believe in you, and that's that.'

Then something odd happened.

The colour drained from his wife's face, and her eyes bulged like globes.

'Mildred, my dear,' the Still-Alive Headmaster said, 'whatever is the matter? You look like you've seen a—'

'Jonathan,' his wife said, 'look!'

The Still-Alive Headmaster turned, following his wife's gaze. When he saw the sight of a blue summer sky swarming with ghostly schoolchildren, he almost leapt out of his skin. 'What in heaven's name—'

The police woman who'd been holding Amelia by the wrist let go and leapt into a hedge.

'Humphrey,' Amelia gasped, 'who are they? What's going on?'

'Oh, just some friends of mine,' I said, and I smiled.

Phantom children from all of history had come to join the fight against bullying. Ghostly girls in Victorian pinnies skipped across the rooftops with spooky skipping ropes, or played hopscotch in the clouds. Ghostly boys in short trousers, blazers and caps kicked phantom footballs or skidded through the sky on transparent bikes.

'Wonderful!' Amelia cried, clapping her hands.

'I asked the children at Ghost School to help us,' I said, 'and, um, here they are, um, helping!'

The two of us watched as the ghost children wisped around the vans and cars, pressing their frightening faces against the windows. 'Let the children go!' they wailed. 'Set the children free!'

The police officers did what they were told, and the still-alive children laughed and cheered as they stepped back onto the pavement.

As for the schoolteachers and dinner ladies, the meaner ones fled, and the kind ones stayed to greet their new supernatural friends.

'It's time we had a word with the Headmaster,' I said. 'Um, Amelia?'

'That,' Amelia said, 'is the most beautiful sight I have ever seen.'

'Amelia, we have to talk to the

Headmaster, before he decides he dreamt the whole thing.'

The air was so thick with ghosties we couldn't see him at first, but then Amelia spotted him trying to climb over the wall of a nearby garden.

'Not so fast,' I said. 'Amelia has something to say, and you'd better listen, or we'll haunt you for the rest of your life.'

The Still-Alive Headmaster lowered himself to the pavement, and stood with his back to the garden wall.

'You're nothing but an overgrown bully,' I said, and I opened another can of fizzy pop.

'This school,' Amelia said, pointing at the red-brick building, 'deserves a headmaster who cares about the pupils. We demand that you resign and promise us that you will never work in education again.'

'No!' the Still-Alive Headmaster cried, and

he pulled his hairpiece down over his eyes. 'This cannot be!'

The Still-Alive Headmaster stumbled away from the wall and into the arms of his wife, and the ghost children wisped around them in a circle, faster and faster, flitting this way and that as they called the Headmaster's name. 'Jonathan!' they called. 'Jonathan! Quit your job or stop being mean!'

'Let me go!' the Still-Alive Headmaster cried. 'I'll do anything. Just leave me in peace.'

'If we let you go,' I said, 'do you promise to do all you can to ensure that this school gets the head teacher it deserves?'

'I promise!' the Still-Alive Headmaster bawled, and he sprinted off down the street, his wife following close behind.

17

The Last Laugh

On Monday, as the still-alive pupils filed into assembly, I wisped into Amelia's satchel. I wanted to hear the new Still-Alive Headmaster's introductory speech.

'You don't need to hide any more, Humphrey,' Amelia said in the corridor.

'There isn't room in this school for a phantom pupil,' I said. 'I think it's best I keep out of sight.'

'You're right,' Amelia whispered. 'The sooner

this school gets back to normal, the better.'

'Amelia, have you seen Humphrey Bump?' a vaporous voice said, and I wisped out of the satchel to find Samuel Spook floating by the assembly-hall door. 'Ah, Humphrey!'

'Samuel,' I said, glancing round at the frightened faces, 'I think we'd better keep out of sight. The sooner this school gets back to normal, the better.'

'Good idea,' Samuel said, and the two of us wisped into Amelia's satchel.

But then we heard a girl's voice say, 'Anyone seen Humphrey?'

'He's in my satchel,' Amelia said, opening the flap.

'Fay and Phil,' I said, peering out. 'Samuel and I are trying to keep out of sight.'

'The sooner this school gets back to normal,

the better.' Samuel told the Phantom twins as they wisped in.

Amelia followed the other pupils into the hall. 'The old headmaster promised he'd find us a decent head teacher,' she whispered. 'Let's hope he's kept his word.'

'No one can be as bad as that mean-spirited bully,' I whispered back.

But when the new headmaster took to the stage, we had the shock of our lives.

The new headmaster was Wither.

'Hush, please!' Wither wailed, waving his willowy arms. 'Remain quiet, or you won't be able to hear my poem.'

I wisped out of Amelia's satchel, followed by Samuel and the twins.

'Oh, what have we done?' Amelia said.

I shrugged. 'It looks like that old bully has had the last laugh after all.'

Amelia looked at me and smiled. 'Wither's poetry can't be that bad. Um, can it?'

'It's worse than bad,' Samuel said, and the twins laughed.

'Put these in your ears,' I said, and I handed Amelia two strawberry marshmallows.

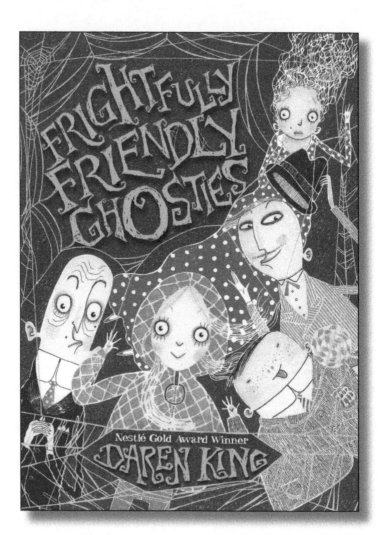

Nestlé Gold Award Winner
DAREN KING

Frightfully Friendly Ghosties

Daren King
Illustrations by David Roberts

'This story is exciting, charming and ridiculous' *Guardian*

'Incredibly funny and imaginative' *Sunday Express*

'A sweetly bizarre tale about cooperation and friendship that should enchant ghoulish children' *Literary Review*

Tabitha Tumbly, Charlie Vapour, Rusty Chains and their ghostly friends can't understand why the still-alives in their house are so mean. When Pamela Fraidy gets locked in the attic by a still-alive, the ghosties are determined to make friends with them.

But the friendlier the ghosties are, the meaner the still-alives become. Whenever the ghosties try to talk to them, the still-alives rush out of the room shrieking!

When the still-alives start putting nasty garlic around the house and then call in a priest, Tabitha and Charlie decide to call The Ghoul to sort out the still-alives once and for all . . .

The lovable characters, brilliant one-liners and the clever plot will delight children and their parents.

FRIGHTFULLY FRIENDLY GHOSTIES
Ghostly Holler-Day
Nestlé Gold Award Winner
DAREN KING

Frightfully Friendly Ghosties
Ghostly Holler-Day

Daren King
Illustrations by David Roberts

'Will leave young readers wanting more' *Books for Keeps*

It's winter, and what could be better than a ghostly holler-day by the sea? But how are Tabitha Tumbly, Charlie Vapour, Humphrey Bump and the other ghosties to decide between Frighten-on-Sea and Scare-borough?

A postcard from their friend Headless Leslie decides for them: Headless is in Frighten and cannot remember how to get home.

So the friends set off on an exciting ghostie caper involving a haunted Frighten pier, a funfair and a mysterious phantom magician. But will it all end in spooky fun or devilish disaster?